D0500683

Introduction

This cookbook is more than just a book of recipes. It's about bringing us all closer through food. It's a Small World has been a beloved part of the Disney Parks for many years. But the idea of it is still all about the way we live today—sharing our lives, our traditions, and our favorite foods.

The Small World characters will show you how to make some fun dishes—and that will help you get to know a little about people in other countries. When you taste chocolate mousse, you might say "Ooh la la!" just like someone who lives in France. A tasty quesadilla might make you want to find out more about Mexico. It's fun to learn about the many traditions of the world, and what better way to do that than through food?

This cookbook has a lot to look at and to make, but the most important ingredient of all is this: a donation has been made in support of the book that will help **FEED** give Vitamin A to children who need it most. Vitamins help kids grow up strong and healthy. But some of the world's poorest children don't get the food or vitamins they need. The Vitamin A supplements that **FEED** will be able to give kids will help them fight against measles and pneumonia. It will even help them fight against losing their eyesight.

FEED's mission is to help **FEED** the world. We're proud to be part of a book that brings our small world closer together.

But now it's time to get going! So pick a recipe, gather your ingredients, and remember to ask an adult to help you in the kitchen. And have fun cooking up some traditions of your own.

Lauren Bush

CEO & Co-Founder
FEED Projects

FEED
OUR SMALL WORLD
A Cookbook for Kids

Disney PRESS
New York

Table of Contents

BONJOUR BREAKFASTS

BREAKFAST

5

C'est Magnifique Quiche Serves 8

The best part about making quiche is you can choose whatever meat and veggie fillings you like, although it tastes especially good with bacon and spinach.

FRANCE

Ingredients

Premade pie shell, baked and cooled
2 tablespoons vegetable oil
1 large onion, chopped
1 clove garlic, minced
6 to 8 ounces spinach leaves, stemmed
   and coarsely chopped
3 large eggs

1 ⅓ cups half-and-half or whole milk
1 teaspoon Dijon mustard
½ teaspoon salt
¼ teaspoon ground black pepper
4 strips cooked bacon, crumbled
2 cups grated cheddar cheese

Directions

1 Heat the oven to 375°F. Meanwhile, ask an adult to help you heat the vegetable oil in a large skillet over medium heat and sauté the onion until it is clear, about 8 minutes. Stir in the garlic and spinach. Cover the pan to steam the vegetables until tender, about 4 minutes, stirring once or twice. Remove the skillet from the heat.

2 Whisk the eggs in a large bowl. Blend in the half-and-half, mustard, salt, and pepper. Spread the cooked vegetables evenly in the pie shell and sprinkle on half of the bacon and the cheese. Ladle the egg mixture over the filling and sprinkle on the remaining cheese.

3 Bake the quiche on the center oven rack until slightly puffy and golden brown (about 40 to 45 minutes). Cool the quiche in the pan on a wire rack for at least 30 minutes before serving, and refrigerate any leftovers.

oeuf
egg

The world's biggest quiche took eighteen hours to bake and was made of almost 2,000 eggs!

If you've ever had *churros*, which are fried dough sticks sprinkled with cinnamon and sugar, you probably had them for dessert. But Spaniards almost always eat them for breakfast and dip them in hot chocolate!

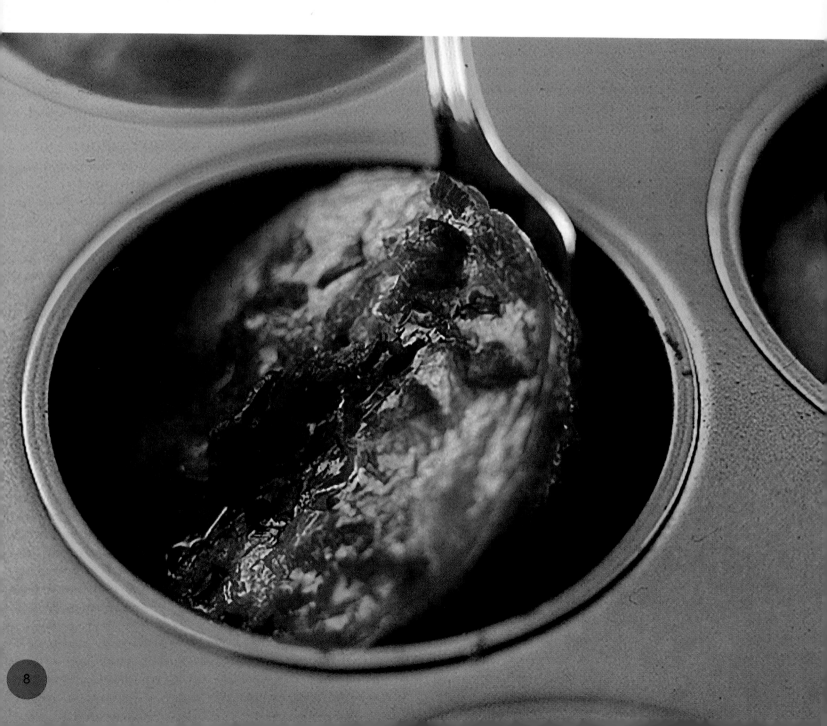

SPAIN

Morning Fiesta Mini Frittatas Makes 6

A frittata is a lot like an omelet, except you don't have to flip it over. Instead of cooking one big frittata, you can use a muffin pan to make individual-size ones. That way everyone gets to choose the mix-ins they like best.

Ingredients

4 large eggs
¼ cup half-and-half
½ teaspoon salt
Assorted mix-ins (such as shredded cheese, diced vegetables or cooked potatoes, and crumbled bacon or chopped ham)

queso
cheese

Directions

1 Ask an adult to help you heat the oven to 350°F. Coat a 6-cup muffin pan with nonstick cooking spray.

2 Whisk together the eggs, half-and-half, and salt in a medium bowl. Then evenly divide the egg mixture among the muffin cups.

3 Add about 2 tablespoons of mix-ins to each cup. Sprinkle them with a bit of Parmesan cheese, if you like.

4 Bake the frittatas until they are puffy and the edges are golden brown, about 20 to 25 minutes. If necessary, run a butter knife around the edge of each one to loosen it before removing it from the pan.

Jammin' Jammy Scones Serves 8

Scottish scones, which are also called bannocks, have been around for hundreds of years. Some Scots make their scones with raisins, cheese, or even potatoes!

SCOTLAND

Ingredients

3 cups flour
½ cup sugar
2 teaspoons baking powder
½ teaspoon baking soda
1 teaspoon salt

14 tablespoons cold unsalted butter,
  cut into small pieces
1 cup low-fat buttermilk
¼ cup of your favorite jam

Directions

1 Heat the oven to 425°F. In a large bowl, combine the first 5 ingredients. Ask an adult to help you use a pastry cutter or two knives to cut the butter into the flour mixture until the mixture resembles coarse cornmeal. Stir in the buttermilk.

2 Use your hands to gather the dough into a ball and place it on a lightly floured surface. Pat the dough into a rectangle about 1 inch thick. Don't handle it too much or the scones will be too dense.

3 Spread jam on half of the rectangle. Fold the plain half over the half with the jam. Now roll the dough into a long rectangle about ¾ inch thick.

4 Cut the dough into 12 squares and place them ½ inch apart on an ungreased cookie sheet. Bake the scones for 14 to 15 minutes.

Griddle scones, which are part of a full Scottish breakfast, are fried instead of baked. Which isn't surprising, because Scottish people like to deep-fry everything. Fish, chips (which we call french fries), chicken—even pizza and candy bars!

Belgium isn't just famous for its waffles; it's famous for its chocolate, too! For a special Belgian treat, try putting chocolate syrup on your waffles.

Snappy Gingerbread Waffles Makes 14

Flavored with molasses and yummy spices, these waffles taste great with or without a topping.

BELGIUM

Ingredients

4 eggs
⅓ cup sugar
1 cup molasses
1 cup buttermilk
3 cups flour
2 teaspoons ground ginger

1 ¼ teaspoons cinnamon
1 teaspoon ground cloves
¾ teaspoon salt
2 teaspoons baking soda
2 teaspoons baking powder
½ cup unsalted butter, melted

Directions

1 Ask an adult to help you use an electric mixer to beat the eggs until they are light and fluffy, about 2 minutes. Add the sugar, molasses, and buttermilk. Beat the mixture for 1 more minute.

2 In a separate bowl, sift together the flour, spices, salt, baking soda, and baking powder. Stir the dry ingredients into the egg mixture just until the batter is smooth. Stir in the butter.

3 Ask an adult to help you cook the batter in a waffle iron until the waffles are golden brown, about 2 to 4 minutes.

Streusel-rific Coffee Cake Serves 8

GERMANY

One of the things that makes German muffins and cakes taste so good is the sweet streusel on top. In this recipe, some of the cinnamon topping is swirled right into the batter.

Ingredients

COFFEE CAKE

2 cups flour
1 teaspoon baking powder
½ teaspoon baking soda
½ teaspoon salt
¼ cup sugar
1 tablespoon butter, melted
1 egg, at room temperature
1 ½ cups buttermilk, at room temperature

TOPPING

⅓ cup brown sugar
½ cup chopped pecans or walnuts
2 teaspoons cinnamon

Directions

1 Ask an adult to help you heat the oven to 375°F. Butter a 9-inch cake pan with 2-inch sides and dust it with flour.

2 In a large mixing bowl, combine the first 5 ingredients. In a medium-size bowl, combine the butter, egg, and buttermilk.

3 Stir the buttermilk mixture into the flour mixture until the batter is evenly mixed. Pour the batter into the prepared pan.

4 Mix together the topping ingredients and sprinkle them evenly over the batter. Run a knife or spoon through the batter to swirl some of the topping into the cake. Don't overdo it, though—you don't want to mix it in too much.

5 Bake the coffee cake until a toothpick inserted in the middle comes out clean, about 25 to 30 minutes. Serve the coffee cake warm.

There is a huge festival every year in Germany called Oktoberfest. Food—from sausages (*wurstl*) to pretzels (*brezn*)—is a big part of the celebration.

16

Fruity and Nutty Muesli Serves 3

Muesli is usually mixed with milk or yogurt a few minutes before you eat it.
Some people like to mix it the night before and keep it chilled until breakfast.

SWITZERLAND

Ingredients

1 cup plain nonfat yogurt
1 cup quick oats
½ cup whole almonds, walnuts, or pecans
1 tablespoon flaxseed meal (optional)
1 tablespoon maple syrup or honey
1 cup fresh berries

Directions

1   Ask an adult to help you use a blender to combine the yogurt, oats, nuts, flaxseed meal, and maple syrup or honey.

2   Blend the mixture until the oats and nuts are in small pieces, about 30 seconds.

3   Spoon the muesli into bowls and top it with the berries. Or you can blend half of the berries into the muesli and use the rest for garnish.

honig
honey

blaubeere
blueberries

LICKETY-SPLIT LUNCHES

19

Cheddar Cheese-tastic Soup Serves 6

Of all the types of cheese that are found around the world, cheddar is an all-time favorite—especially the extrasmooth and creamy cheddar made in the Canadian province of Ontario. No wonder it's the star ingredient in this hearty soup.

Ingredients

2 tablespoons butter
¼ to ⅓ cup grated carrot
¼ cup minced onion
¼ cup finely chopped celery
2 tablespoons flour
¼ teaspoon nutmeg

3 cups chicken broth
½ cup half-and-half
8 ounces cheddar cheese, grated
  (about 2 to 2 ½ cups)
1 teaspoon Worcestershire sauce

Directions

1 Ask an adult to help you heat a heavy saucepan. Melt the butter and sauté the carrot, onion, and celery in it until tender, about 4 minutes.

2 Add the flour and nutmeg, and cook the mixture for another minute, stirring the whole time. Gently whisk in the chicken broth and bring it to a simmer. Cover the pan and cook the broth for 15 minutes. Remove the pan from the heat.

3 Add the half-and-half and cheddar cheese to the pan, stirring continually until the cheese melts. Stir in the Worcestershire sauce and serve the soup with bread or crackers.

Did you know that cheese sweats? As it ages, the proteins in cheese release moisture. It's all part of the process that makes cheddar and other hard cheeses so flavorful.

In some parts of India, food at weddings is served on banana leaves instead of plates!

Easy Pita Pockets Serves 4 to 6

Like many Indian dishes, this recipe gets its zip from adding curry powder. So what exactly is curry powder? It's a blend of toasted spices, such as coriander, cumin, turmeric, cinnamon, cloves, and dried chilies.

INDIA

Ingredients

½ cup mayonnaise
½ cup sour cream
1 tablespoon lemon juice
2 to 3 teaspoons curry powder
½ teaspoon Dijon mustard
3 cups cooked, cubed chicken breast

¾ cup halved green grapes
½ cup chopped roasted cashews
Salt and ground black pepper to taste
2 or 3 pita breads
Leaf lettuce

Directions

1 First make the dressing by blending the mayonnaise, sour cream, lemon juice, curry powder, and mustard in a small bowl.

2 In a large bowl, combine the chicken, grapes, and cashews. Stir in the dressing until everything is well mixed. Add salt and pepper to taste.

3 To assemble the sandwiches, halve the pita breads and place a couple of leaves of lettuce in each half. Spoon in the chicken salad and serve.

Wrap 'n' Roll Wraps Serves 4

In Greece, gyros are usually made with pita bread, roasted meat, and *tzatziki* sauce—which is made from yogurt, cucumbers, and spices.

GREECE

Ingredients

1 cup plain yogurt
1 cup crumbled feta (about 4 ounces)
¼ cup chopped red onion
2 teaspoons lemon juice
4 (10-inch) flour tortillas
2 cups cooked, shredded chicken
2 tomatoes, sliced
2 cups salad greens

Directions

1 In a small bowl, mix together the yogurt, feta, onion, and lemon juice for the dressing.

2 To make each wrap, heat a tortilla in the microwave for 10 seconds. Spread about ⅓ cup of the dressing on the tortilla, staying about an inch away from the edge. Layer on ½ cup of the chicken, several tomato slices, and salad greens. Fold the sides of the tortilla toward the center. Then fold up the bottom to cover the filling and roll the tortilla snugly.

3 Tightly wrap each sandwich in plastic and refrigerate it for up to 6 hours. Cut the gyros in half at serving time.

κρεμμύδι
onion

μαρούλι
lettuce

 **FUN FACT**

Greek families celebrate the New Year by making *diples* for dessert. *Diples* are fried dough strips drizzled with honey and sprinkled with chopped nuts and cinnamon.

25

For a sweet treat, Cuban empanadas can be made with a fruit filling, such as apple, pineapple, pear, or even pumpkin.

CUBA

Warm and Toasty Empanadas   Makes 12

In Cuba, kids love to eat tasty little meat turnovers called empanadas for lunch. They're fun to make, too—especially when you crimp the edges together with a fork to seal in the filling.

Ingredients

2 tablespoons olive oil
1 medium onion, finely chopped
2 tablespoons minced fresh parsley
8 ounces cooked ham, chopped
2 tablespoons bread crumbs
8 ounces mild cheddar or Jarlsberg, shredded
2 tablespoons sour cream

1 large egg, lightly beaten
Pinch of ground black pepper
1 package empanada wrappers or 2 packages frozen puff-pastry shells, thawed and rolled into 5-inch circles
Egg wash (made from 1 lightly beaten large egg combined with 1 tablespoon of water)

Directions

1   Ask an adult to help you heat the oil in a skillet over medium heat and sauté the onion and parsley in it, stirring occasionally, until the onion is clear, about 3 minutes. Transfer the mixture to a medium bowl and set it aside until cool.

2   Add the ham, bread crumbs, cheese, sour cream, egg, and black pepper to the bowl, and mix the ingredients well.

3   For each empanada, place 2 heaping tablespoons of filling in the center of an empanada wrapper or puff-pastry shell. Lightly moisten the edge of the circle with the egg wash. Fold the wrapper (or pastry) in half, firmly pressing the edges together. Use a fork dipped in flour to crimp the edge and pierce the top (so steam can escape). Chill the empanadas for 30 minutes.

4   Heat the oven to 375°F. Brush the turnovers with the egg wash and bake them on a parchment-lined baking sheet placed on the top oven rack until they turn golden brown, about 20 to 25 minutes. Let the empanadas cool for a few minutes before serving.

CHINA

Sensational Sesame-Soy Noodles Serves 6

For a little challenge, try eating these tasty noodles with chopsticks!

Ingredients

8 ounces Chinese egg noodles or pasta
  noodles (such as linguini or angel hair)
3 tablespoons dark sesame oil
3 tablespoons low-sodium soy sauce
2 tablespoons rice vinegar
2 tablespoons honey
⅛ to ¼ teaspoon ground ginger

Dash of salt
Dash of ground black pepper
1 red bell pepper, thinly sliced
½ cup grated carrot
2 to 4 medium scallions, thinly sliced
½ cup grated daikon radish (optional)

Directions

1 Bring a medium pot of water to a boil over
   high heat. Add the noodles whole (do
   not break them into shorter pieces) and
   cook them until tender, about 5 to 7
   minutes. Stir the noodles occasionally
   while they cook to keep them from
   sticking together.

2 Meanwhile, in a small bowl, whisk
   together the sesame oil, soy sauce, rice
   vinegar, honey, ground ginger, salt, and
   ground black pepper.

3 When the noodles are done, drain them and transfer them to a serving bowl. Add the
   bell pepper, carrot, scallions, and radish. Pour on the sauce and toss everything well.
   Serve the noodles warm or chilled.

FUN FACT

Chinese noodles can be made from wheat, rice, or beans, and they come in all different widths. Dragon-beard noodles, for instance, are so thin they would quickly dissolve if you cooked them in water. Instead, they are fried in oil and served crispy.

Tropical fruits are used in lots of Thai recipes, including pickled mango, mango ice cream, pineapple jam, and pineapple candy.

Chicken, Pineapple, and Mango Tango Serves 4

This fresh and fruity salad makes a perfect lunch on a warm summer day.

Ingredients

1 (14-ounce) can regular or light coconut milk
1 tablespoon Thai red curry paste
2 teaspoons freshly grated orange zest
½ cup fresh-squeezed orange juice
4 boneless, skinless chicken breasts, cut into
 1-inch chunks
1 mango, peeled, pitted, and cut into 1-inch
 chunks

1 large egg, lightly beaten
Pinch of ground black pepper
1 package empanada wrappers or 2 packages
 frozen puff pastry shells, thawed and rolled
 into 5-inch circles
Egg wash (made from 1 lightly beaten large
 egg combined with 1 tablespoon of water)

Directions

1 In a bowl, whisk together the coconut milk, red curry paste, orange zest, and orange juice. Reserve ½ cup of the mixture in a separate container.

2 In a sealed ziplock plastic bag, toss together the chicken breast chunks and half of the marinade from the bowl. Toss the fruit and the remaining marinade in another ziplock plastic bag. Let the food marinate at room temperature for 15 to 30 minutes. Then thread the chicken and fruit pieces onto separate skewers.

3 Ask for an adult's help to grill the chicken, turning it once, until it is cooked through, about 3 to 4 minutes per side. Grill the fruit skewers for about 2 minutes per side.

4 Remove the grilled meat and fruit from the skewers and serve them over salad greens drizzled with the reserved marinade from step 1. (Be sure NOT to use the leftover marinade from the ziplock bags the raw chicken and fruit were in!)

Zesty Peanut Soup Serves 6

Everyone knows that peanut butter goes well with jelly, chocolate, and celery. But it's also an important ingredient in this soup from Senegal!

SENEGAL

Ingredients

1 tablespoon vegetable oil
1 medium onion, chopped (about 1 ½ cups)
1 carrot, grated (about ½ cup)
1 large sweet potato, peeled and grated
   (about 3 cups)
3 cups water
1 (10.75-ounce) can condensed tomato soup

½ cup creamy peanut butter
1 teaspoon curry powder
⅛ to ¼ teaspoon cayenne pepper
½ cup sour cream (optional)
2 tablespoons chopped peanuts,
   for garnish (optional)

Directions

1 Ask an adult to help you heat the oil in a large saucepan over medium heat. Add the onion and the carrot and sauté until tender, about 3 to 5 minutes.

2 Add the sweet potato and the water, then cover and simmer for 10 minutes or until the sweet potato is soft. Stir in the condensed soup, peanut butter, curry, and ⅛ to ¼ teaspoon of cayenne pepper (depending on the level of spiciness your family prefers), then bring the mixture to a boil. Remove the pan from the heat and let cool for 10 minutes.

3 With an adult's help, puree the soup in a blender in 2 batches (or use a handheld immersion blender), then return it to the pan and reheat it. Ladle the soup into bowls and, if you like, top it with a dollop of sour cream and a few chopped peanuts.

In Senegal, peanuts are called "groundnuts," and so many farmers in Senegal grow them that some people call it the peanut capital of the world!

DELIZIOSO DINNERS

DINNER

Today's Special

Spectacular Spaghetti and Meatballs Serves 8

Spaghetti and meatballs go together like peanut butter and jelly. But it wasn't until immigrants came to America that the two were served together!

ITALY

Ingredients

1 cup crumbled Italian bread
¼ cup water
1 ½ pounds ground beef
2 eggs
1 cup freshly grated Parmesan cheese
1 ½ teaspoons finely chopped garlic

¼ cup finely chopped fresh parsley
1 ½ teaspoons salt
Freshly ground black pepper to taste
2 tablespoons olive oil
2 (28-ounce) jars tomato sauce
1 pound spaghetti

Directions

1 In a small bowl, soak the bread in the water. Then gently squeeze the bread and discard the excess water.

2 Transfer the moistened bread to a large bowl. Add the ground beef, eggs, cheese, garlic, parsley, salt, and pepper. Stir the mixture with a wooden spoon until it is well combined, then shape it into 2-inch balls.

3 Ask an adult to help you heat the oil in a large, deep saucepan over medium heat. Cook the meatballs in batches, turning them with tongs, until they are nicely browned, about 10 minutes (they will finish cooking in the sauce).

4 Heat the tomato sauce in a large saucepan until it begins to simmer. Add the meatballs and let them simmer in the sauce, turning them occasionally, until they are cooked through, about 10 minutes.

5 Cook and drain the spaghetti. Spoon some of the sauce into a large warmed serving bowl. Add the spaghetti, and toss well to keep it from sticking together. Serve the spaghetti with the meatballs and additional sauce.

Colomba Pasquale, which means "Easter Dove," is a special dessert made by Italians for Easter. It is shaped like a dove and topped with almond slices and sugar.

In Japan it is considered bad manners to spear food or point at someone with your chopsticks!

Chicken-or-the-Egg Rice Bowl Serves 4 to 6

Rice is part of almost every meal in Japan. In this tasty dish, the rice is topped with chicken stir-fry.

JAPAN

Ingredients

1 tablespoon vegetable oil
4 chopped scallions
1 cup chicken broth
½ cup grated carrots
2 cups baby spinach

2 tablespoons sugar
¼ cup soy sauce
4 breaded and cooked chicken cutlets,
   cut into strips
5 large eggs, beaten
4 cups cooked rice

Directions

1 Ask an adult to help you heat the vegetable oil in a large skillet over medium-high heat. Add the chopped scallions and sauté them for 2 to 3 minutes. Stir in the chicken broth, and let mixture simmer for 2 minutes.

2 Add the grated carrots and baby spinach, stirring until the spinach has completely wilted. Stir in the sugar and soy sauce.

3 Add the chicken and simmer for 3 more minutes.

4 Pour the eggs over the chicken. Let the mixture simmer, stirring occasionally, until the eggs are cooked through, 8 to 10 minutes.

5 Serve the chicken mixture spooned over the cooked rice.

Peanutty Beef Satay Serves 4

INDONESIA

Satay, which is made by grilling pieces of seasoned meat on a stick, is so popular in Indonesia it's sold everywhere from street carts to fancy restaurants. Once cooked, the meat is often dipped into a spicy peanut sauce and served with pickles.

Ingredients

SATAY

1 pound flank steak, trimmed
3 tablespoons fresh lime juice
2 tablespoons soy sauce
1 tablespoon Asian fish sauce
2 teaspoons dark brown sugar
2 garlic cloves, minced
½ teaspoon curry powder
⅛ teaspoon crushed red pepper
Bamboo skewers, soaked in water for 30 minutes

PEANUT SAUCE

1 tablespoon canola oil
¼ cup minced shallots
2 garlic cloves, minced
¾ teaspoon Thai red curry paste
⅓ cup creamy peanut butter
2 tablespoons hoisin sauce
2 teaspoons dark brown sugar
⅔ cup water
1 tablespoon fresh lime juice

Directions

1 To make the satay, ask an adult to slice the meat in half lengthwise and then cut it across the grain into thin ¼-inch strips. (Tip: Partially freezing the meat for 45 minutes will make it easier to slice.)

2 Whisk the lime juice, soy sauce, fish sauce, dark brown sugar, garlic, curry powder, and crushed red pepper in a medium bowl. Gently toss the steak in the satay sauce. Cover the bowl and set it aside at room temperature for 30 minutes.

3 Meanwhile, make the peanut sauce. Ask an adult to help you heat the oil in a small saucepan, and sauté the shallots, garlic, and Thai red curry paste for about 3 minutes. Stir in the peanut butter, hoisin sauce, dark brown sugar, and water. Bring the mixture to a boil and simmer for 1 minute. Stir in the lime juice.

4 When the steak is ready, thread 2 to 3 pieces onto each skewer, stretching them flat so they will cook evenly.

5 Ask an adult to grill the skewered steak until it is seared and just cooked through, about 2 minutes per side. Serve the satay with the peanut sauce.

Many Indonesians eat with a spoon in their left hand and a fork in their right—although plenty of people eat with their hands!

Painting? Sculpture? Tea-making? In Morocco, brewing mint tea—the most popular drink—is considered an art form!

Kickin' Chicken Stew Serves 4 to 6

MOROCCO

Cinnamon, cloves, and raisins make this stew spicy and sweet—perfect for a cold winter night.

Ingredients

STEW

1 tablespoon vegetable oil
1 small onion, chopped
2 to 3 cloves garlic, minced
½ teaspoon turmeric
¼ teaspoon cinnamon
3 whole cloves
2 bay leaves
2 cups chicken broth
4 skinless, boneless chicken thighs
  (about ¾ to 1 pound)
1 (14.5-ounce) can whole tomatoes with juice
1 large carrot, sliced

1 ½ cups green beans, snapped into
  smaller pieces
1 small summer squash, quartered and
  cut into large chunks
1 (15.5-ounce) can chickpeas, drained and rinsed
½ teaspoon salt
⅓ cup golden raisins

TOPPING

2 cups chicken broth
1 cup water
1 ½ cups Moroccan couscous

Directions

1 You'll need an adult to help you use a Dutch oven or large (8-quart) pot to heat the oil over medium heat for 1 to 2 minutes. Add the onion and garlic and sauté them for 2 minutes. Stir in the turmeric, cinnamon, cloves, and bay leaves. Cook the mixture for 2 to 3 minutes.

2 Add the chicken broth, chicken thighs, and tomatoes with juice. Bring the stew to a boil and then reduce the heat and simmer it, covered, for 25 minutes.

3 Stir in the carrots, green beans, squash, chickpeas, and salt. Continue cooking the stew with the cover on for another 10 minutes, stirring occasionally and breaking the chicken and tomato chunks into smaller pieces. Add the raisins. Keep simmering the stew, covered, until the vegetables are tender, about 10 minutes more.

4 To make the couscous, bring the broth and water to a boil in a saucepan. Quickly stir in the couscous. Remove the pan from the heat and cover it. Let the couscous set for 5 minutes. Then fluff it with a fork.

5 Spoon a mound of couscous into each serving bowl. Ladle the stew around the couscous.

MEXICO

Caliente Veggie Quesadilla Serves 1

A quesadilla is sort of like the Mexican version of a grilled cheese sandwich, but instead of using bread, you melt the cheese inside a folded tortilla. Even better, you can add other ingredients—like veggies and salsa.

Ingredients

¼ cup grated carrot
¼ cup cooked and chopped broccoli
1 tablespoon chopped yellow or Vidalia onion (optional)
⅓ cup shredded Monterey Jack or cheddar cheese
½ teaspoon canola oil
1 10-inch (burrito-style) flour tortilla
1 tablespoon salsa or taco sauce

Directions

1 In a medium bowl, mix together the carrot, broccoli, onion, and cheese.

2 Lightly coat the bottom of a large nonstick frying pan with the canola oil. With the help of an adult, set the pan over medium heat.

3 Place a tortilla in the pan, cover it with the veggie-and-cheese mixture, and drizzle salsa or taco sauce on top.

4 When the bottom of the tortilla is lightly browned and the cheese has melted, fold the quesadilla in half and transfer it to a plate. Cut the quesadilla into quarters and serve it hot.

Did you know that the word "chocolate" comes from Mexico? The Aztecs used it to make a drink called *xocoatl*, which is kind of like hot cocoa.

FUN FACT

46

Super Shepherd's Pie Serves 6 to 8

IRELAND

This traditional Irish supper is a complete meal in one pan: a layer of seasoned ground meat and diced carrots topped with creamy mashed potatoes and bubbling cheese. If you like, you can swap the carrots for corn.

Ingredients

¾ cup milk
1 cup quick oats
1 tablespoon beef soup mix
  (or a crushed bouillon cube)
1 egg, lightly beaten
1 tablespoon onion flakes
2 teaspoons parsley
¼ teaspoon thyme

¼ teaspoon ground black pepper
1 cup diced, cooked carrots (or raw grated)
1 pound lean ground beef
4 cups hot mashed potatoes
1 teaspoon onion powder
8 ounces grated cheddar cheese

Directions

1 Ask an adult to help you heat the oven to 350°F. Meanwhile, mix together the milk, oats, soup mix, and egg in a large bowl. Add the onion flakes, parsley, thyme, pepper, carrots, and beef. Mix well.

2 Press the mixture into a large pie plate and bake it for 45 minutes. Meanwhile, mix the potatoes with the onion powder.

3 Remove the meat from the oven and ask an adult to help you drain the grease. Sprinkle the meat with most of the cheese. Then spoon the potatoes on top and dot them with the remaining cheese.

4 Broil the pie until the potato peaks start to brown and the cheese melts.

Perfect Paella Serves 8

SPAIN

This popular rice dish tastes especially good when you make it with chorizo, a Spanish smoked sausage — but, if you like your food a little less spicy, you can also make it with kielbasa, a Polish smoked sausage.

Ingredients

1 tablespoon olive oil
1 whole chicken, cut into 8 pieces, or 4 legs
  and 4 thighs
Salt and pepper
16 ounces sausage (preferably chorizo)
  cut into half-moon slices
1 small onion, finely chopped
1 red bell pepper, finely chopped
2 garlic cloves, chopped

2 cups medium-grain rice
½ teaspoon cumin
½ teaspoon salt
Pinch of saffron
1 cup seeded and chopped tomato
4 cups chicken stock
½ cup frozen peas

Directions

1 Ask an adult to help you heat the oven to 400°F and to help you heat the oil in a large skillet over medium-high heat. Sprinkle the chicken with salt and pepper and place it in the skillet to brown, about 4 to 5 minutes on each side (you can cook it in batches if there's not enough room). Set the browned chicken aside on a plate.

2 Now lightly brown the sausage in the skillet, about 3 to 4 minutes. Add the sausage to the plate with the chicken.

3 Drain all but 1 tablespoon of fat from the pan, and lower the heat to medium. Sauté the onion, red pepper, and garlic, stirring occasionally, until they are tender, about 6 minutes. Stir in the rice, cumin, salt, and saffron, and cook the mixture for about 1 minute.

4 Spoon the rice and vegetable mixture into an oiled 9- by 13-inch baking dish. Arrange the chicken and sausage on top of the rice and then scatter on the tomato. Place the pan on the center oven rack and carefully pour the chicken stock over the meat and rice.

5 Bake the paella for 25 minutes. Then sprinkle the peas on top and let it cook until the liquid is absorbed, another 10 to 15 minutes. Cool the paella for at least 10 minutes before serving.

Saffron is the spice that gives many Spanish stews and rice dishes their golden yellow color. It comes from the part of the crocus flower that pollen sticks to, and it takes thousands of flowers to make just one ounce of saffron.

DREAMY DESSERTS

51

ITALY

Dolce Ricotta Pie Serves 8 to 10

Made with a mild, soft, white Italian cheese, this lemony pie is as delicious as cheesecake but lighter and a little less creamy.

Ingredients

PIE SHELL

5 tablespoons butter, melted
⅓ cup sugar
1 ⅔ cups graham cracker crumbs
  (about 18 crushed squares)
Dash nutmeg

FILLING

½ cup sugar
3 tablespoons cornstarch
1 teaspoon baking powder
1 container (16-ounce) ricotta cheese
½ cup light cream
2 large eggs
1 teaspoon vanilla extract
½ teaspoon grated lemon zest
1 teaspoon lemon juice
2 to 3 tablespoons graham cracker crumbs

Directions

1 Heat the oven to 350°F. Meanwhile, make the pie shell by stirring together the butter, sugar, and 1 cup of the graham cracker crumbs in a bowl until well mixed. Press the cracker mixture into a pie plate and bake the shell for 6 to 8 minutes. Then set it on a wire rack to cool.

2 For the filling, whisk together the sugar, cornstarch, and baking powder in a mixing bowl. Add the ricotta, cream, and eggs. Beat the mixture with an electric mixer until smooth.

3 Beat in the vanilla extract, lemon zest, and lemon juice.

4 Pour the filling into the pie shell and sprinkle the graham cracker crumbs on top.

5 Bake the pie until it is firm around the edges (the center will still be a bit soft), about 50 to 55 minutes. Then chill it before serving.

Another Italian dessert made with ricotta cheese is cannoli. Cannoli can be coated with chocolate, sprinkled with chocolate chips, or dusted with powdered sugar.

FUN FACT

At Christmastime, Polish families eat a dessert called *makowiec*. This cake has a dark filling that looks like chocolate—but it's actually made of poppy seeds!

54

Tummy-Tempting Thumbprint Cookies Makes about 4 dozen

POLAND

If you're looking for a cookie that's as much fun to make as it is to eat, this Polish treat wins thumbs down. No kidding. You actually use your thumb to make a dent in the middle so you can fill it with your favorite jam.

Ingredients

1 cup unsalted butter, softened
½ cup packed brown sugar
1 large egg
1 teaspoon vanilla extract

3 cups flour
½ teaspoon salt
Granulated sugar for rolling the cookies in
½ cup jelly or jam

cukier
sugar

Directions

1   Place the butter and sugar in a large bowl. Ask an adult to help you use an electric mixer to beat the mixture until light and fluffy. Then beat in the egg and vanilla extract.

2   Combine the flour and salt, and gradually stir them into the butter and egg mixture. Cover and chill the dough until it is firm enough to roll into balls (1 to 2 hours).

3   Ask an adult to help you heat the oven to 350°F. Form the dough into 1-inch balls and roll them in a bowl of granulated sugar. Place the balls on ungreased baking sheets about 2 inches apart.

4   Press deeply into the center of each cookie with your thumb. If a cookie cracks, just press the dough together again. Fill each indentation with ½ teaspoon of jelly or jam.

5   Bake the cookies until they are lightly browned, about 10 to 12 minutes. Cool them on the baking sheets for about 2 minutes. Then use a spatula to transfer the cookies to a wire rack to cool completely.

Mousse au Chocolat Serves 4 to 6

In French, the word *mousse* means foam—a perfect description of this creamy dessert that will literally melt in your mouth.

FRANCE

Ingredients

5 tablespoons confectioners' sugar
1 ¼ cups heavy cream
5 ounces semisweet chocolate
1 ounce unsweetened chocolate
1 teaspoon vanilla extract

Directions

1   Place a metal mixing bowl in the refrigerator to chill (you'll use this for whipping the cream later). In a small heavy saucepan, stir 4 tablespoons of the confectioners' sugar into ¼ cup of the heavy cream. Break both of the chocolates into pieces and add them to the pan. Ask an adult to help you heat the mixture over low heat, stirring all the while, until the chocolate melts and the ingredients are well combined.

2   Remove the pan from the heat and stir in the vanilla extract. Pour the chocolate mixture into a large mixing bowl and set it aside until it is cool yet still fluid.

3   Whip the remaining 1 cup of cream and 1 tablespoon of confectioners' sugar in the chilled metal bowl until soft peaks form (don't overdo it or you'll end up with butter).

4   Fold the whipped cream into the chocolate until evenly combined. Spoon the mousse into dessert dishes and enjoy, or chill it until serving time.

One popular French pastry is called "napoleon," but this has nothing to do with Napoleon Bonaparte! The name actually comes from the French word *napolitain*, which refers to the Italian city of Naples.

Ruth Wakefield actually invented chocolate chip cookies by accident! When she ran out of baking chocolate, she used tiny bits of semisweet chocolate, thinking the pieces would melt into the dough. Good thing they didn't!

Chocolate Chip Cookie Pie Serves 8 to 10

This pie is like one huge chocolate chip cookie!

UNITED STATES

Ingredients

1 unbaked 9-inch piecrust
½ cup butter, softened
¾ cup packed brown sugar
2 large eggs
2 tablespoons maple syrup
⅔ cup flour
1 cup semisweet chocolate chips
½ cup chopped walnuts (optional)

Directions

1 Ask an adult to help you heat the oven to 350°F. Meanwhile, using an electric beater, cream the butter and sugar in a large mixing bowl. Beat in the eggs and maple syrup until the mixture is light and fluffy. Then beat in the flour. Stir in the chocolate chips and nuts.

2 Spread the filling in the piecrust. Bake the pie for 50 minutes, covering it with aluminum foil if the top starts to get too brown. When done, a knife inserted between the edge and the center of the pie should come out clean.

3 Cool the pie for 15 minutes and serve it warm, topping each slice with a scoop of ice cream, if desired.

JAMAICA

Island Breeze Ginger Cake Serves 9

There's no skimping on the ginger in this spicy Jamaican dessert. Sweetened with molasses and brown sugar, it's rich, moist, and really delicious!

Ingredients

2 cups flour
1 teaspoon baking soda
½ teaspoon salt
2 teaspoons ground ginger
1 teaspoon cinnamon
1 teaspoon ground allspice
1 teaspoon ground nutmeg
1 teaspoon ground cloves

½ cup butter, softened
½ cup packed brown sugar
½ cup molasses
2 tablespoons peeled and finely grated
   fresh ginger
1 large egg
⅓ cup hot water

Directions

1   Ask an adult to help you heat the oven to 350°F. Lightly butter an 8-inch-square baking pan and dust it with flour.

2   In a medium bowl, whisk together the flour, baking soda, salt, and the 5 dry spices.

3   In a large mixing bowl, use an electric mixer to cream the butter and sugar. Beat in the molasses and grated fresh ginger. Then beat in the egg.

4   Beat half of the flour mixture into the butter mixture. Add the water and beat again. Finally, add the remaining flour mixture and beat just until mixed in.

5   Spread the batter in the prepared pan and bake it until a toothpick inserted in the middle comes out clean, about 30 to 35 minutes. Cool the cake in the pan on a wire rack for 15 minutes. Then remove the cake from the pan to finish cooling.

Jamaican ice cream is actually made with coconut milk instead of cream. One of the most popular flavors? Grape nut!

The British word for "dessert" is "pudding," and one of the most famous British puddings—sticky toffee pudding—is made by covering a warm sponge cake with toffee sauce. Yum!

Buttery Shortbread Makes 4 ½ dozen cookies

Sometimes you feel like chocolate, and sometimes you don't! This recipe lets you decide if you want to make chocolate or almond-flavored shortbread.

ENGLAND

Ingredients

1 cup unsalted butter, at room temperature
¾ cup confectioners' sugar
⅓ cup unsweetened cocoa powder,
   or ⅓ cup ground blanched almonds
¼ teaspoon salt
2 cups all-purpose flour
1 egg white (optional)
¼ cup chopped almonds (optional)

Directions

1 Ask an adult to help you use an electric mixer to cream together the butter, sugar, cocoa powder (or ground almonds), and salt.

2 Add the flour, mixing just until incorporated.

3 Divide the dough into three equal pieces and roll them into logs. Wrap each log in wax paper and put them in the refrigerator for 2 hours.

4 With an adult's help, preheat the oven to 325°F. Remove the dough from the refrigerator and unwrap one log. Cut slices of dough ¼-inch thick and place them on a cookie sheet. Bake for 6 to 10 minutes, or until cookies are firm but not brown. Repeat with the other two logs.

5 If you'd like to add an extraspecial touch, a couple minutes before the cookies are done, take them out of the oven, brush them with egg white, and sprinkle chopped almonds on top. Then continue baking until the cookies are done.

Acknowledgments

Our heartfelt thanks go out to the staff of Disney *FamilyFun* magazine,
who created the recipes and photographs that fill this book.
Special gratitude to Deanna Cook and Jean Cranston.
Recipes edited by Cynthia Littlefield, who also created, photographed,
and styled the recipes on pages 20, 52, 56, 58, and 60.

Illustrated by Nancy Kubo
Designed by Winnie Ho

FEED® and the FEED Logo are used with permission of FEED Projects LLC, and such marks constitute
registered and common law trademarks or service marks of FEED Projects LLC.

A donation has been made in support of the cookbook that will enable
the FEED Foundation to provide Vitamin A supplements to 450,000 children for one year.
A year's supply of Vitamin A for one child costs just two cents.

Disney *FamilyFun* is a division of Disney Publishing Worldwide. For more great ideas and to
subscribe to Disney *FamilyFun* magazine, visit FamilyFun.com or call 1-800-289-4849.
Printed in the United States of America
First Edition
10 9 8 7 6 5 4 3 2 1
ISBN 978-1-4231-4779-4
G942-9090-6-11182
For more Disney Press fun, visit www.disneybooks.com